Michael

Retirement confirm

Great Escaper,, Reasons behind his
retirement, Biography, Early Life, Career,
Marriage, Recognition and Net Worth

By

Bert Rivers

Table of contents

Biography

Sir Michael Caine, an English film actor, gained recognition for his outstanding and critically acclaimed performances in films such as "Zulu" (1964), "The Italian Job" (1969), "Get Carter" (1971), "Educating Rita" (1983), and more recently, "Batman Begins" and "The Dark Knight." He received knighthood from Queen Elizabeth II in 2000 as a tribute to his significant contributions to the world of cinema.

Caine was born as Maurice Joseph Micklewhite in Rotherhithe, South East LondonMarch 14, 1933. His parents were Ellen Frances Marie, who worked as a cook and charlady, and Maurice Joseph Micklewhite, a fish market porter.

He was previously married to actress Patricia Haines from 1955 to 1958, and they had one daughter named Dominique. In 1968, he had a romantic relationship with Bianca Jagger. Caine has been happily married to actress and model Shakira Baksh since January 8, 1973. Their connection began when Caine saw her in a Maxwell House coffee commercial and a friend provided him with her phone number. They share a daughter named Natasha.

The actor who clinched two Academy Awards has an extensive movie career that spans seven decades, encompassing timeless classics like Zulu and The Italian Job, as well as contemporary blockbusters such as Interstellar and The Dark Knight trilogy.

Renowned British actor, Sir Michael Caine, has officially announced his retirement from acting following the release of his most recent film. This decision comes after a distinguished career that earned him Oscars, Golden Globes, and Bafta awards for his roles in over 160 films during a career that spanned seven decades.

In his final movie, "The Great Escaper," which hit theaters on October 6, Sir Michael shares the screen with the late Glenda Jackson, who passed away in June after the film's completion. In this film, he portrays the real-life Second World War veteran Bernie Jordan, who escaped from a care home to attend D-Day celebrations in France.

Recognitions and Achievements:

He received the Academy Award in 2000 and 1987 for Best Actor in a Supporting Role.

He was honored with the Golden Globe Award in 1999 for Best Actor in a Motion Picture - Musical or Comedy, in 1989 for Best Actor in a Limited Series or Motion Picture Made for Television, and in 1984 for Best Actor in a Motion Picture - Musical or Comedy.

Category: Arts & Culture

In Detail: Sir Michael Caine

Birth Name: Maurice Joseph Micklewhite, Jr.

Date of Birth: March 14, 1933, in London, England (currently aged 90)

Awards and Recognitions:

- Academy Award (2000) for Best Actor in a Supporting Role
- Academy Award (1987) for Best Actor in a Supporting Role
- Golden Globe Award (1999) for Best Actor in a Motion Picture - Musical or Comedy
- Golden Globe Award (1989) for Best Actor in a Limited Series or Motion Picture Made for Television

- The Golden Globe Award in 1984 for Outstanding Actor in a Musical or Comedy Film.

Career

In "The Italian Job" film, the actor formerly known as Maurice Micklewhite adopted his screen name from the 1954 movie "The Caine Mutiny." His acting career began in 1953 on stage and progressed to motion pictures in 1956. He played diverse roles in various British productions like "A Hill in Korea" (1956), "How to Murder a Rich Uncle" (1957), "The Day the Earth Caught Fire" (1961), and "Zulu" (1964). His success commenced with "The Ipcress File" (1965), the first of five films where he portrayed British spy Harry Palmer. However, his true breakthrough was in the lead role of "Alfie" (1966), which earned him an Academy Award nomination for Best Actor.

In these early films, Caine demonstrated his versatility, effectively embodying characters ranging from cynical secret agents and charismatic playboys to rugged adventurers and refined gentlemen. His amiable Cockney persona remained a constant, and he skillfully infused subtly humorous elements into his performances.

By the 1970s, Caine achieved international stardom with roles in movies like "Get Carter" (1971) and an Oscar-nominated performance in "Sleuth" (1972), where he acted alongside Laurence Olivier. He continued to star in popular films like "The Man Who Would Be King" (1975) and "The Eagle Has Landed" (1976). Throughout the

1980s, he appeared in numerous films, both successful and less so, earning a reputation as a dedicated and hardworking actor.

In the 1980s, his notable films included "Dressed to Kill" (1980), "Educating Rita" (1983) with an Oscar nomination for Best Actor, "Hannah and Her Sisters" (1986) with an Academy Award for Best Supporting Actor, and "Dirty Rotten Scoundrels" (1988). By the end of the 20th century, Caine had amassed a filmography of more than 100 movies. He won his second Best Supporting Actor Oscar for "The Cider House Rules" (1999) and received a Best Actor nomination for "The Quiet American" (2002).

Caine's later roles included portraying Alfred, the butler and confidant of Batman, in Christopher Nolan's "Batman Begins" (2005) and its sequels. He appeared in other notable films like "Children of Men" (2006), "The Prestige" (2006), and Kenneth Branagh's remake of "Sleuth" (2007).

Throughout the 2010s, Caine's roles ranged from a vigilante in "Harry Brown" (2009) to a corporate spy mentor in "Inception" (2010). He lent his voice to animated films such as "Gnomeo & Juliet" and "Cars 2," and acted in movies like "Journey 2: The Mysterious Island," "Now You See Me," and "Interstellar." Caine also starred in "Youth" (2015), "Going in Style" (2017), "King of Thieves" (2018), and "Tenet" (2020). In 2021, he appeared in "Best Sellers."

Additionally, Caine authored successful books, including "Acting in Film" (1987), considered a valuable resource for actors, and his memoirs "What's It All About?"

(1993) and "The Elephant to Hollywood" (2010). He received several honors, including Commander of the Order of the British Empire (CBE) in 1993, knighthood in 2000, and Commander of the Order of Arts and Letters in 2011, the highest cultural honor in France.

Early Life

Michael Caine, originally named Maurice Joseph Micklewhite, was born on March 14, 1933. His father, Maurice, and his mother, Ellen Frances, along with his brother Stanley and maternal half-brother David (deceased), were part of his family. Growing up in London, he faced the challenges of a poor, working-class upbringing in rough neighborhoods. To steer clear of street trouble, he joined a local youth club and discovered his passion for acting, ultimately deciding to pursue it as a career. He honed his acting skills through various club activities and, after completing high school, began working as a clerk and messenger in a film company.

At 19, Michael Caine had to pause his acting aspirations when he was drafted into national service. After spending two years abroad, he returned to London in 1954, joined a repertory company, and secured minor roles in their productions. For the following decade, he endured a series of small parts in film, television, and repertory, all while maintaining his determination. In 1964, he achieved a breakthrough when he landed a supporting role in the well-received film "Zulu." This movie catapulted him to fame, leading to leading roles in blockbusters like "The Ipcress File" (1965) and "Alfie" (1966), which gained him recognition in both the UK and Hollywood.

Financially, Sir Michael Caine boasts a net worth of $75 million, primarily stemming from his highly successful acting career. Caine's journey since his breakthrough in the 1960s has been marked by appearances in critically acclaimed films like "Funeral in Berlin," "The Italian Job," "Sleuth," "Dressed to Kill," "Educating "Raising Rita," "Mona Lisa," "Hannah and Her Sisters," "The Dark Knight Trilogy," "Inception," "Interstellar," and "Now You See Me." His illustrious career has earned him numerous awards, including two

Oscars. Awards for Best Supporting Actor in 1987 and 2000.

Marriage and Family

Michael Caine's marital journey includes two unions. His first marriage was to the late Patricia Haines, a well-known English actress. They met at a Suffolk theater and exchanged vows on April 3, 1954, but the marriage concluded after eight years with a divorce in 1962. Caine later acknowledged that the marriage ended due to his immaturity, particularly his difficulty in coping with his wife's greater success at the time.

His second opportunity at love came with model/actress Shakira Caine. The story goes that he first saw her in a television commercial, captivated by her beauty and determined to meet her. Leveraging his showbiz connections, he managed to obtain her contact information. After persistent effort and initial resistance, she agreed to a date. They ultimately began dating and sealed their relationship with a Las Vegas wedding in 1973. Over the years, they have built a strong and enduring partnership, becoming a celebrated couple in Hollywood. Caine's wife often accompanies him to red carpet events and film locations, which he mentions is to help him resist the allure of beautiful actresses.

In terms of family, Caine has two daughters: Dominique from his first marriage and Natasha Haleema from his second.

Michael Caine's Physical Attributes

Michael Caine stands at a height of 6 feet 2 inches (1.88 meters) and weighs 86 kilograms. His hair has turned gray over the years, and his eyes are a striking shade of blue. Despite his age, Caine remains lively and agile, crediting his strong work ethic and healthy lifestyle for his longevity. He avoids sugar and salt in his diet and is a non-smoker.

Retirement

The two-time Academy Award-winning actor, renowned for a prolific career spanning seven decades with iconic movies like Zulu and The Italian Job, as well as recent blockbusters such as Interstellar and The Dark Knight trilogy, has officially retired from acting. British actor Sir Michael Caine, celebrated with Oscars, Golden Globes, and Bafta awards, made this announcement after a career that included more than 160 films.

His final film, "The Great Escaper," released on October 6th, featured Sir Michael alongside the late Glenda Jackson. In it, he portrayed the real-life Second World War veteran Bernie Jordan, who escaped from a care home to attend D-Day celebrations in France.

Sir Michael expressed his retirement decision, saying, "I keep saying I'm going to retire. Well, I am now. I've realized that I've already had a lead role with fantastic reviews, and I'm unlikely to get more lead roles at 90 or 85. It's best for me to exit while I'm ahead.

In 2021, he initially contemplated retirement after starring in the film "Best Sellers" due to health issues affecting his mobility and a lack of acting offers. He ultimately accepted the role in "The Great Escaper" after initially turning it down three times.

Sir Michael's retirement coincides with the release of his debut novel, "Deadly Game," fulfilling his long-standing ambition to write a thriller.

Category:

Title: "Wealth and Background of Michael Caine"

- Total Net Worth: $60 Million
- Date of Birth: Born on March 14, 1933 (Currently 90 years old)
- Place of Birth: Hails from Rotherhithe
- Gender: Male
- Height: Stands at 6 feet 2 inches (1.88 meters)
- Profession: Multifaceted roles as an Actor, Author, Film Producer, Voice Actor, and Entrepreneur
- Nationality: Proudly represents the United Kingdom
- Michael Caine, the acclaimed English actor and writer, has accumulated a net worth of $60 million. He has earned his reputation as one of the highest-grossing figures in the history of the box office. His journey to stardom began in the 1960s, and over the

years, he has garnered numerous career accolades and awards.

Real Estate Deals:

- In 2008, Michael acquired a newly constructed Miami condominium for $4.07 million, later selling it in January 2018 for $7.45 million.
- In 1999, Michael and his spouse invested 1 million pounds in an 8-acre estate located 1.5 hours outside of London. In early 2019, they listed this property for sale at $5 million.

Quick Michael Caine Facts:

- Full Name: Michael Caine
- Total Wealth: $75 Million
- Birth Date: March 14, 1933

- Birthplace: Rotherhithe, London, United Kingdom
- Height: Stands at 6 feet 2 inches (1.88 meters)
- Professions: Versatile roles as an Actor, Author, Film Producer, Voice Actor, and Entrepreneur
- Education: Attended Wilson's School and Hackney Downs School
- Nationality: Proudly representing the United Kingdom
- Spouses: Married Shakira Caine in 1973 and was previously married to Patricia Haines from 1955 to 1962
- Children: Natasha Caine, Dominique Caine
- Parents: Ellen Maria Burchell, Maurice Joseph Micklewhite
- Siblings: Stanley Caine, David Burchell

- Nicknames: Known by various names including Maurice Joseph Micklewhite, Michael Scott, Maurice Micklewhite, Sir Michael Caine, Sir Michael Caine CBE
- Awards: Knighted by Queen Elizabeth II in 2000 for his exceptional contributions to cinema
- Nominations: Received nominations for BAFTA, Golden Globe Award for Best Actor, Variety Club Awards, and Academy Award
- Notable Movies: Includes "The Ipcress File" (1965), "Alfie" (1966), "Sleuth" (1972), "Educating Rita" (1983), "Hannah and Her Sisters" (1986), "The Cider House Rules" (1999), and "The Quiet American" (2002)

- TV Shows: Appeared in shows such as "Jack the Ripper" (1988), "Jekyll & Hyde" (1990), "World War II: When Lions Roared" (1994), and "Mandela and de Klerk" (1997)

Printed in Great Britain
by Amazon

34440951R00020